LiLA the FAiR

by Laura Driscoll
illustrated by Blanche Sims

Kane Press, Inc.
New York

Text copyright © 2005 by Kane Press, Inc. Illustrations copyright © 2005 by Blanche Sims.

All rights reserved. No part of this book may be reproduced or transmitted in any form
or by any means, electronic or mechanical, including photocopying, recording, or by any
information storage and retrieval system, without permission in writing from the publisher.
For information regarding permission, write to Kane Press, Inc., 240 West 35th Street,
Suite 300, New York, NY 10001-2506.

Library of Congress Cataloging-in-Publication Data

Driscoll, Laura.
  Lila the Fair / by Laura Driscoll ; illustrated by Blanche Sims.
     p. cm. — (Social studies connects)
  "Civics - grades: 1–3."
  Summary: Lila is so effective at settling her sisters' arguments
she decides to serve as peacemaker at school as well.
  ISBN 1-57565-148-3 (pbk. : alk. paper)
  [1. Sisters—Fiction. 2. Reconciliation—Fiction. 3.
Schools—Fiction.] I. Sims, Blanche, ill. II. Title. III. Series.
  PZ7.D79Li 2005
  [Fic]—dc22
                              2004016961

10 9 8 7 6 5 4 3 2 1

First published in the United States of America in 2005 by Kane Press, Inc.
Printed in Hong Kong.

Social Studies Connects is a trademark of Kane Press, Inc.

Book Design: Edward Miller

www.kanepress.com

I slam my book shut and cover my head with a
pillow. How can I read with all that racket? Rose
and Allie are at it again. "What are you two arguing
about this time?" I yell.

My little sister, Allie, rushes to one side of my bed. "Lila," she whines, "Rose called me a name."

My big sister, Rose, plops down on the other side. "It's true," Rose says with a smirk. "I did."

I'm the one in the middle, and just like always, I'm stuck in the middle of my sisters' fight.

This is a job for Lila the Fair.

Fair means that things have been made equal in some way.

4

Lila the Fair is what my dad calls me when I act as the family peacemaker—which happens a lot.

I do try to be fair. Sometimes I think Allie is being a baby, like when she cried because Rose touched her doll.

Sometimes I think Rose is being mean, like when she wouldn't let Allie use her yo-yo.

Either way, I try to call it like I see it.

Did you ever disagree with someone? Maybe you each had different needs, wants, or ways of thinking. That's called a **conflict**.

Most of all, I wish Rose and Allie would get along. What's so hard about that?

"What name did Rose call you?" I ask Allie.

"She called me a mammal," Allie whines.

Rose bursts out laughing. I give her a look and turn to Allie.

"All humans are mammals," I explain. "Rose didn't call you a *bad* name."

Allie sniffs. "Oh," she says. Then she skips away, as if nothing has happened. Rose plops onto the floor and flips through a magazine.

What Lila just did is called **conflict resolution**. Lila figured out how to settle her sisters' disagreement peacefully.

Yes! Lila the Fair has done it again. I always feel good when I find a way to settle my sisters' arguments. It's like solving a puzzle. I almost wish I could find more people with more arguments—more puzzles I could solve!

Hey! That gives me an idea.

The next day at school, I tack a flyer to the notice board. My friend Chad sees me and comes over. "What are you up to?" he asks.

"Just doing my part for school peace," I say.

ARE YOU HAVING A SQUABBLE? TIFF? QUARREL? LET LILA BROWN SETTLE YOUR

LOST

FAMILY MOVIE NIGHT

DID YOU KNOW?
There's a special prize for peacemakers! It's called the Nobel Peace Prize and it's given every year to a person who has worked for world peace. Some of the winners are: Dr. Martin Luther King, Jr.; Mother Teresa; and President Jimmy Carter.

Chad scrunches up his face. "Why do you want to be bothered with other people's fights?" he asks.

"It won't be a bother," I say. "It'll be a snap!"

After all my practice with Rose and Allie, I bet I could settle arguments in my sleep!

ARE YOU HAVING A...
SQUABBLE ?
TIFF ?
QUARREL ?
SPAT ?

LET LILA BROWN SETTLE
YOUR NEXT DISPUTE!
SHE'S EXPERIENCED.
SHE'S FAIR.
SHE'S FREE!
NO ARGUMENT TOO BIG
OR TOO SMALL.
GET IT SETTLED...

ASK LILA THE FAIR!

Lila the Fair

News travels fast. I get my first official job at lunchtime.

Lucas and Mike walk over to my table. They're both holding onto a paper plate with a chocolate-nut brownie on it.

"Lila, you're hired," says Lucas.

"Yeah," Mike says. "We need help settling something. This is the last brownie. Lucas and I reached for it at the same time."

"So who gets it?" Lucas asks.

I smile at Chad, who is sitting next to me.

"That's easy," I say. I pick up a plastic knife and cut the brownie in half. "Split it," I tell them. "It's only fair!"

Both Lucas and Mike look disappointed. Then Mike shrugs. "It's not what I wanted you to say," he says. "But it *is* fair."

They each take a brownie half and walk away.

"See?" I say to Chad. "A snap!"

DON'T WAIT—MEDIATE!
Suppose you are having trouble settling a conflict. You can ask a third person to help. Someone who helps both sides settle their differences is called a **mediator**. Sometimes a mediator comes up with a brand-new solution!

At recess the next day, two groups of kids come up to me. The third graders want to use the field to play soccer. The second graders want to use it to play kickball. "We got here first," says a second grader.

"But they used it yesterday," argues a third grader.

I'm a third grader, myself. But Lila the Fair doesn't play favorites!

"Play against each other," I tell them. "That way, everyone gets to use the field. And flip a coin. Heads, it's kickball. Tails, it's soccer."

They all seem okay with that.

More satisfied customers. Boy, am I good!

A good mediator doesn't take sides. He or she tries to be fair to everyone.

Soon it seems like everyone has an argument for me to settle. Sam and Seth Myers are twins. They are fighting over Otis, their pet iguana.

"Have you tried making an iguana schedule?" I ask them.

Sam and Seth think that over.

"Oh," says Sam. "You mean, I play with Otis Mondays, Wednesdays, and Fridays—"

"And I get him Tuesdays, Thursdays, and Saturdays!" says Seth. "But what about Sundays?"

Hmm . . . That's a tricky one. But I have an idea.

"Iguana's day off?" I try.

Sam and Seth look at each other and nod.

TIME OUT!
Do you ever feel too upset or angry to resolve a conflict? Take some time to calm down. It's much better to *talk* about a problem than to *yell* about it!

In art class, Tommy and Brenda are fighting over what color to make their monster.

"Red!" shouts Tommy.

"Blue!" shouts Brenda.

"Striped!" I suggest. Problem solved!

BE WISE—COMPROMISE!
In a **compromise**, each person gives up something to get something he or she wants. A red-and-blue striped monster is a compromise!

After school, Eric and Kevin try to trick me.

"We're having a fight over which came first—the chicken or the egg," Kevin says.

"Chicken!" shouts Eric. "It laid the egg!"

"Egg!" yells Kevin. "Or else, where did the chicken come from?"

"Nice try, guys!" I say. "But that's a question nobody has ever been able to answer."

At ballet, I notice Jenna and Ruthie sitting at opposite ends of the bench. Jenna and Ruthie are best friends. They sit next to each other in class. They eat lunch together. They take ballet together.

But now they are not speaking!

"Is something the matter?" I ask them.

"Ruthie's not a good
friend," Jenna says. "She told
Ben Davis that I like him. And it was a secret!"

"So?" Ruthie says to Jenna. "*You* went to
Alma's house without asking me to go, too."

They both look surprised. Then they look at
me for an answer. But I don't have one. "I'll get
back to you," I say.

Right up until bedtime I keep thinking about
Jenna and Ruthie. But I can't come up with an easy
way to settle their argument. It doesn't help that my
sisters are at it again in the other room.

"Rose," Allie whines, "stop breathing so loudly!"

I try to ignore them. The way I see it, Jenna and Ruthie hurt each other's feelings. They both did something wrong. But telling them that won't fix their friendship.

What can I say that will settle their argument?

I go to bed and have a terrible dream. I'm a chocolate-nut brownie. I'm being pulled in two directions—by Sam and Seth's iguana on one side, and Tommy and Brenda's monster on the other. I'm about to be split right down the middle!

I wake up tangled in my blankets. It's morning. *Whew!* It was just a bad dream.

Then I realize I still don't have an answer for Jenna and Ruthie.

Lila the Fair has failed.

At ballet that afternoon, I walk over to Jenna and Ruthie. "About your fight—"

"Oh, never mind," Jenna says.

"Yeah," says Ruthie. "We made up."

"Huh?" I say.

Ruthie nods. "Before yesterday, I didn't know why Jenna was mad at me."

"And I didn't know why Ruthie was mad at me," Jenna explains. "But after we spoke to you, we talked it all out."

"Yeah, we were both wrong," says Ruthie. "But now we're best friends again!"

"Thanks, Lila!" Jenna says.

WALK IN SOMEONE ELSE'S SHOES!
Sometimes arguments start because one person doesn't understand another's way of thinking, or **point of view**. It helps to put yourself in the other person's place.

So everything worked out, after all. I couldn't settle Jenna and Ruthie's argument for them. They had to settle it themselves, and they did. I feel happy about that.

But I can't stop thinking about that dream I had. Maybe being Lila the Fair at home is enough for one peacemaker.

"Allie!" I hear Rose call out as I open our front door. "Your epidermis is showing!"

"It is not!" Allie whines.

Ah, yes. My work here is never done.

EPIDERMIS
Top layer of skin

And, as for the kids at school . . . I'll just help them help themselves!

31

I can resolve conflicts!

MAKING CONNECTIONS

Do you ever have disagreements over who gets the last cookie, or the next turn on the slide? Everyone has conflicts. The trick is to find a way to resolve them without fighting.

As Lila finds out, conflicts do not have easy answers—but they can still be resolved with a little hard work!

Look Back

- Who is having a conflict on pages 3 and 4? What is the conflict about? How does Lila resolve it on page 6?
- On page 11, what is the conflict between Lucas and Mike? How does Lila settle it? Is her solution fair? Why?
- Look at page 14. What is the conflict? Does Lila take sides in the argument? On page 15, what is her solution? Do you think it's a good one? Why?
- What does Lila observe on page 20? What does she ask Jenna and Ruthie? On page 27, how do Jenna and Ruthie say they resolved their problem?

Try This!

Be a mediator! Look at the pictures. How would you resolve each conflict? (Hint: Check Lila's poster on page 31.)